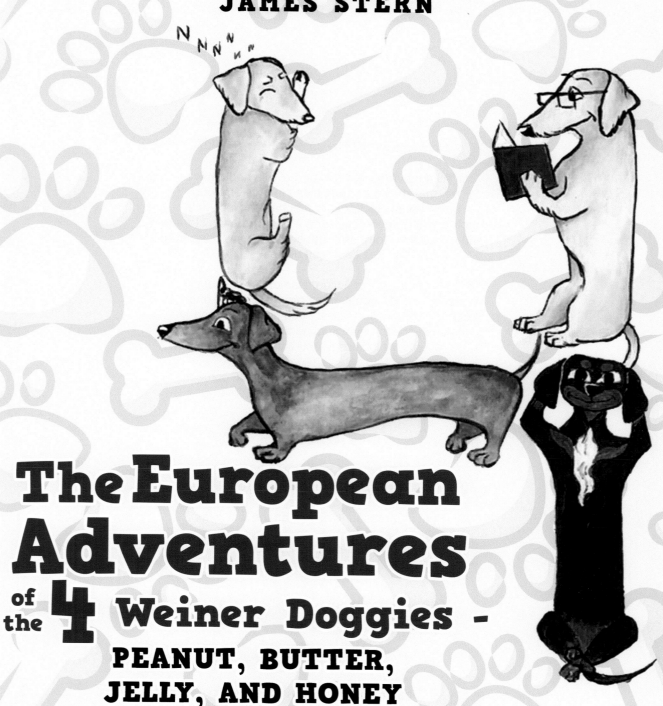

To order additional copies of this book, contact:
Xlibris
844-714-8691
www.Xlibris.com
Orders@Xlibris.com

ISBN: 978-1-6698-6246-8 (sc)
ISBN: 978-1-6698-6247-5 (e)

Print information available on the last page

Rev. date: 01/23/2023

The European Adventures of the 4 Weiner Doggies -
Peanut, Butter, Jelly, and Honey

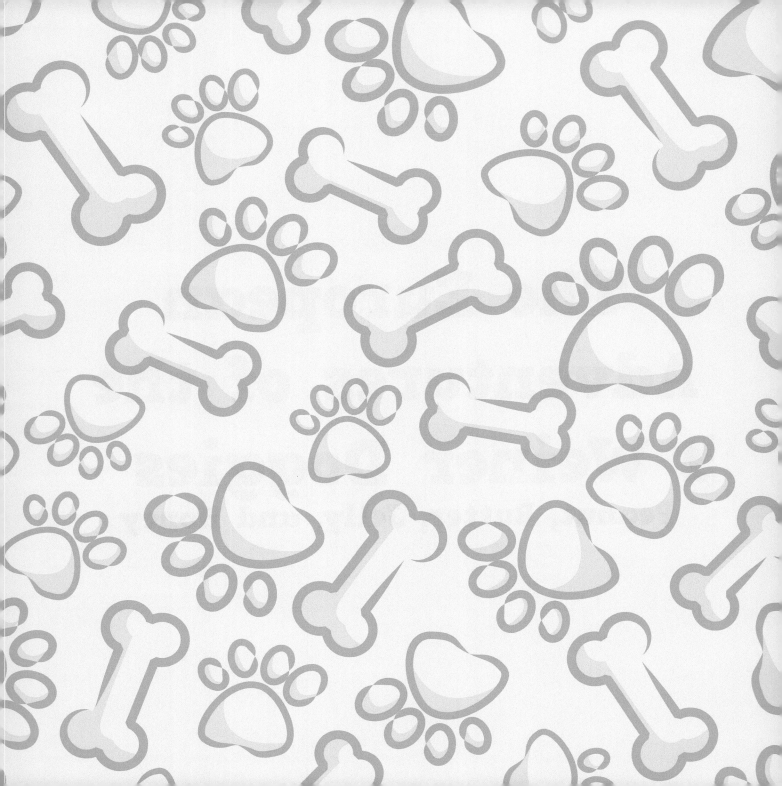

Chapter One

Peanut, Butter, Jelly, and Honey are so excited to finally go on vacation together!! They have never been on an airplane before. Honey wants to bring her pajamas so she can sleep on the airplane. Peanut, Butter, and Jelly share one suitcase and Honey has one large suitcase all to herself. Honey is very fashionable and stuffs her suitcase full of her favorite clothing. Honey also thinks she can sneak some extra doggie treats on the airplane when nobody is watching – Silly Honey!

When they arrive at the airport, Peanut, Butter, Jelly and Honey are confused by all the people walking around them. They all decide to start barking to clear the way. Honey just smiles and everyone blows her kisses
— Silly Honey!

Chapter Two

Peanut, Butter, Jelly, and Honey are sitting in their seats on the airplane. They don't like to be apart they would rather cuddle together in one seat. They all move to Peanut's seat and hide under a blanket.

But Honey sees a pretty little kitty cat sitting in First Class and sneaks up there when nobody is watching to bring her a treat!

Later during the airplane ride, Butter gets super hungry, so she looks around for an extra doggie bone until dinner time. Honey is sweet enough to share some of her treats with everyone.

Chapter Three

Peanut, Butter, Jelly, and Honey arrive in London, England and immediately find a place to eat Fish and Chips!

While they are eating, Honey enjoys talking to Hanna the English Cocker Spaniel and Olivia, the Manchester Terrier. Hanna and Olivia tell Honey that everybody should visit the King at Buckingham Palace!

Peanut, Butter, Jelly, and Honey go to Buckingham Palace and are so happy to see how beautiful it is!!

They are wondering if they can go inside and have afternoon tea and cookies with the King! Honey brings a pack of Oreo Cookies just in case Buckingham Palace is out of cookies – Silly Honey!

Chapter Four

Peanut, Butter, Jelly, and Honey love France!

While walking in a park, Peanut, Butter, Jelly, and Honey meet Marie the French Poodle and Louis the French Bulldog, Ooh la la. Marie and Louis are so friendly and nice!! They share their French Bread and Fancy Cheese with Peanut, Butter, Jelly, and Honey!

Honey wants to go shopping in a beautiful Paris boutique with Marie the French Poodle. While they are shopping, Honey picks out a Red Beret and now she thinks she looks like a French Supermodel – Silly Honey!

Louis the French Bulldog takes Butter on a tour of the Eifel Tower. They go to the very top, but Butter prefers the grassy area on the ground where they sell hot dogs.

Peanut and Jelly decide to stay in the hotel and take a nap.

When Honey returns from shopping, she goes to the hotel spa for a full massage treatment.

Chapter Five

Peanut, Butter, Jelly, and Honey arrive in Italy. They meet their Facebook friend Bruno the Big Italian dog. Bruno takes them to his favorite Italian restaurant. Peanut, Butter, and Jelly want a pizza with everything on it. Honey only wants a cheese pizza......

Honey decides to order a plate of spaghetti instead. She slurps it all over her face making a mess – Silly Honey!

Peanut, Butter, and Jelly love walking around Italy looking at all the beautiful trees and mountains. They love the scenery and the Italian clothing. Honey only wants to find an Italian restaurant to eat some more spaghetti – Silly Honey!

Chapter Six

Peanut, Butter, Jelly, and Honey arrive in Germany. In Germany, they see so many Weiner doggies everywhere! They stumble upon a German doggie festival and sing and dance in the streets all day long. They love it here with all their new Weiner doggie friends.

Peanut, Butter, Jelly, and Honey want to eat some German food. They go to a super popular German restaurant with all sorts of German foods.

Butter wants to eat immediately, and she sees a delicious looking long link sausage sitting on a plate at the table next to them. Butter decides to grab the link sausage from the plate when the people are not looking and runs around the restaurant.

Peanut tries to grab the last link of the sausages that Butter is pulling and gets a free ride through the restaurant as Butter looks for the front door.

Honey prefers to munch on her delicious German dessert and not run Around the restaurant and get her outfit dirty – Classy Honey!

Chapter Seven

Peanut, Butter, Jelly, and Honey finally arrive home after their long vacation. Peanut, Butter, and Jelly are sad to leave but can't wait to get home, take a hot bath, eat a treat, and cuddle for bedtime.

Honey only wants to update her Facebook and Instagram accounts before she goes nighty night — Silly Honey!

The girls drift off to sleep dreaming of their next adventure – a beautiful camping vacation.

Printed in the United States
by Baker & Taylor Publisher Services